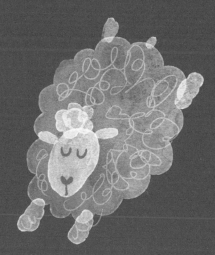
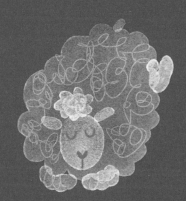

There's a Bear IN YOUR BOOK

Written by TOM FLETCHER

Random House 🏠 New York

For Buzz, Buddy, and Max –T.F.

Copyright © 2022 by Tom Fletcher
Illustrated by Dynamo
Based on illustrations by Greg Abbott

All rights reserved. Published in the United States by Random House
Children's Books, a division of Penguin Random House LLC, New York.
Originally published in paperback in slightly different form by Puffin
Books, an imprint of Penguin Random House Children's Books U.K.,
a division of Penguin Random House U.K., London, in 2022.

Random House and the colophon are registered trademarks of
Penguin Random House LLC.

Visit us on the Web! rhcbooks.com

Educators and librarians, for a variety of teaching tools,
visit us at RHTeachersLibrarians.com

Library of Congress Cataloging-in-Publication Data
is available upon request.
ISBN 978-0-593-70399-1 (trade) — ISBN 978-0-593-70400-4 (ebook)

MANUFACTURED IN CHINA
10 9 8 7 6 5 4 3 2 1
First American Edition

OH DEAR!

It looks like somebody has had a big picnic
in your book. Who could it be?

It's a bear!

A very full bear.

A very full and very tired bear.

This bear needs a good sleep.

Shall we help Bear get ready for bed?

First, Bear needs a bath.
And for a bath you need lots of . . .

Wow!
That's a lot of bubble bath, Bear.

Let's give the book a good **Shake**
to make it super-duper bubbly,
then turn the page.

What a lot of bubbles!
There must be a very clean bear under there.

POP the bubbles . . .

then turn the page.

Well done! Bear is nice and clean.
But your book is very wet—and so is Bear.

What's the best way to dry a soggy bear?
I KNOW!

FLAP your book like a fan
and then turn the page.

WHOOSH!

Well, that certainly got Bear dry!

Now turn the page to get Bear
settled down and snuggled into bed.

SHHH.

Look! Bear's all snuggled up.

GENTLY ROCK the book from SIDE TO SIDE

to lull Bear to sleep.

Well done! Bear is getting sleepier and sleepier.

I'm sure Bear will be asleep
        by the time you turn the page. . . .

BOO!

OH NO! A cheeky little monster
has woken Bear up. Naughty!

Show Monster how upset you are.
Wag your finger at him
and turn the page.

Aw—Monster looks sorry.

How about we let him stay in your book
as long as he helps Bear get to sleep?

Let's make everything comfortable for them.

Can you IMAGINE some soft pillows
and a nice big night-light?

Are you imagining? Good! Now turn the page.

Great imagining!

Now let's make your book
even cozier.

PRESS the switch to turn on Bear's
night-light, then turn the page.

That's better!
Your book feels much cozier now.

And look—
Monster and Bear are settling down for bed.

Now do a big **YAWN!**

I bet that will make
Monster and Bear yawn too....

Great! Monster and Bear are yawning,
but they're not quite asleep.

Hmm . . . a really good way to get to
sleep is to count sheep.

Can you IMAGINE five sheep
for them to count?

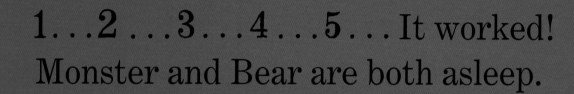

1...2...3...4...5...It worked!
Monster and Bear are both asleep.

But now there are all these
SHEEP in your book!

Can you help them fall asleep too?

Let's sing them a lullaby....

Twinkle, twinkle, little sheep.
Time for you to go to sleep!

SHHHHHH!
Great work! Now everyone's asleep.

Or nearly everyone. . . .

Close the book quickly
before SOMEONE makes a noise!

Sleep tight!